Rescue Me

a short story

ec garrett

For Frankie, who rescued me.

And for all of the animals in shelters around the world waiting for someone to love them. If I could save every single one of you, I would.

Contents

A Warning

The following short story features heavy topics that can be extremely triggering. Please review the trigger warning list before proceeding. If you or someone you know is struggling, I recommend using 988 Lifeline, a free and anonymous service available in the United States where people are available via call/chat/text 24/7/365 to support you. They also have services for those with hearing loss. It's always okay to ask for help.

*Frequently mentioned triggers are in **bold**, and extremely frequent triggers are in **<u>bold and underlined</u>**.*

Mental Health and Suicide

Anxiety & Anxiety Attacks, <u>Depression</u>, Intrusive thoughts, Post Traumatic Stress Disorder, and <u>Suicidal Ideation</u>.

Animal Death and Cruelty

Animal Cruelty & Abuse, **<u>Stressful Shelter Environments</u>,** High-Kill Shelters, Animal Abandonment, and **<u>Animal Suffering</u>.**

EC GARRETT

Foreword

The following story is semi-autobiographical and inspired by my life. The characters and settings are fictional, but there is a thread of reality running through every element, including the animal shelter environment.

Rescue Me is the first story I ever wrote. It's inspired by the hopeless feeling I felt for most of my life and how that changed when a little black and tan dog named Frankie picked me at the shelter. I went into the shelter that day expecting that *I* would choose an animal to rescue, but the moment Frankie saw me, he jumped up on my lap and sat down, facing the room and my parents, as if to say, "She's mine. This is my human. I pick *her*."

Being chosen by an animal is the greatest honor of my life. It also was the best thing I've ever done to help my mental health. Ever since I was a little girl, I have always struggled with extreme anxiety, depression, ADHD, and other mental health related issues.

Frankie truly rescued *me* that day.

More than ten years later, and Frankie is an old man. He brings just as much joy and happiness into my life as he did the day we met. Frankie is my best friend, my child, my forever companion.

As he moves into the end stages of his life, I felt re-inspired to share this story and revisit it. The love he gives me deserves to be told and shared. I rewrote the story from it's original form and then gave it to one of the wonderful editors I'm lucky enough to work with. The final version of Rescue Me is very similar to the first, but with more polish and an extended end sequence.

I hope you enjoy it and remember; there is light at the end of the tunnel.

If you're considering getting an animal, please think about adopting. Shelter animals have so much love to give, and you never know—you might go to rescue a shelter animal and *they* end up rescuing *you*.

XOXO, ECG

Please enjoy the official reading playlist.

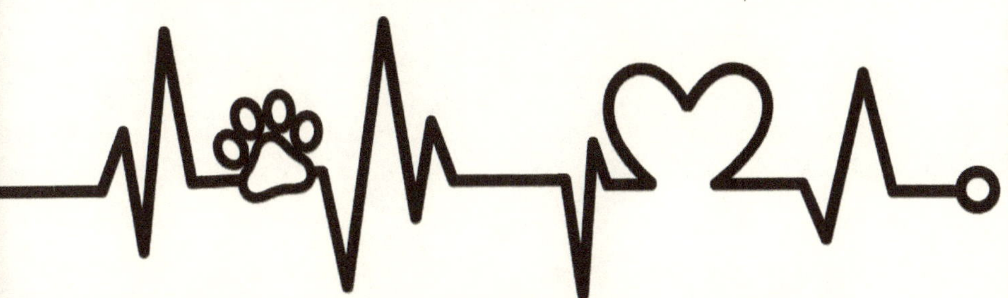

Scan the code to be
taken to the Playlist.

Chapter 1
SAM

I'm so *cold*.

As sleep fades and I begin to wake, my first thought is, "I don't want to wake up."

The cement floor underneath me is uncomfortable and painful, constantly causing my body to ache.

Some of the dogs here have beds, but I overheard the staff talking about how there aren't enough for all of us.

I'm one of the ones who didn't get a bed—one of many.

Every night, I try to huddle into the corner, away from the noise, curling on top of myself to try and get warm. No matter how hard I try to get comfortable, to warm up, it never works—so I've stopped trying.

Shivers are a constant.

I can't remember how long I've been here. I know it has been long enough to forget what a warm bed or a hug feels like. I don't even remember the feeling of a soft blanket against my fur or the taste of a warm meal.

I don't have any memories of my mother or how I got here. I know I was young when I arrived, but I am not young now.

Cries and pleas echo through my tiny prison, coming from my cellmates around me—cries of despair and sadness, cries of pure terror.

The cries always come from the newbies, not knowing what else to do but cry in hopes that someone will let them out. They will realize soon that crying is pointless. Eventually, we all give up crying, give up trying to get the attention of visitors. I gave up a long time ago.

These four walls, this cement floor—this is my life now.

I will never make it out.

I'm older, no longer a bouncing, fluffy pup.

The young ones get the most attention, but the ones who look like me?

We are invisible.

I say there are others, but I only see them when they're taken out on walks or some kind family decides to take them home. They pass my cage, excitement buzzing through their bodies, but I can't bear to look.

It gives me hope when I know I shouldn't have any.

As the cries of my new neighbors get louder, I tuck myself into my corner again, using my dirty, poo-stained tail to cover my nose.

The smell is horrible, but you get used to it.

As I try to go back to sleep, I find myself hoping I won't wake up. I don't want to live through another day like this.

Cold.

Hungry.

Aching.

Hopeless.

Chapter 2
ROSIE

I know it was my idea to come here, but now that we've arrived, doubt and anxiety race through me.

This won't help, I tell myself. Nothing can help, not really. It was a stupid idea; all of my ideas are stupid. No matter how hard I or anyone else tries, these feelings won't go away.

Lonely.

Sad.

Numb.

Hopeless.

The saddest part is that I'm lonely even when I'm not alone, scared even when I should feel completely safe. But it never matters, never makes a difference. No matter how many others are around me or how many times I'm reassured I'm safe, the feelings never go away. They keep eating away at my soul, breaking me into smaller and smaller pieces every day, making it harder for me to ever be put back together again. Sometimes, I go to bed at night hoping I won't wake up; that way, I won't have to keep feeling this miserable.

It's exhausting being sad all the time.

The building in front of me looks like a prison, just a big block of grey cement with one window—the glass on the front door.

Yeah, this was a bad idea. Nothing good could possibly be going on inside a building that looks like this. It looks as miserable as I feel.

I found this shelter on social media, saw a post about how they're completely full and will have to start euthanizing animals to make room.

The idea of that sent me into a spiral. The animals in there don't deserve this fate. They deserve love and happiness.

With a deep breath, I get out of the car.

I called my parents before this, and they tried to reassure me this was a "phenomenal idea." Still, I have doubts.

What if none of them like me? What if they can see how broken I am? What kind of animal wants a broken owner?

I can hear my therapist in my ear, telling me these thoughts are "not based in reality." No matter how much I hear that, it still *feels* real.

The cold air hits my cheeks, making me shiver as I walk towards the front door. A high-pitched jingle goes off when I open the door, and an old woman hands me some paperwork to fill out. I barely have the energy to lift a pen, but I fill out the blank spaces anyway, not looking forward to the long drive back to school with nothing for company but my thoughts.

Listening to music helps, or a podcast. That was a suggestion from my therapist.

When my thoughts get dark, drowning them out with noise helps...*sometimes.* Not always, though.

Handing back the now-filled out papers, the old woman, who, for the record, smells like baby powder and violets (never a good combination) waves her hand to a door behind her for me to go in.

I can hear the high-pitched shrieks and agonized barks from here. My heart starts to race as the nerves fully hit.

"You can do this, Rosie girl," I hear my mom's voice say. *"You're so brave. Just try it. See what happens."*

I don't know if I *can* do this, but I will. For them. For my family and friends who haven't given up on me, even though I've begun to give up on myself.

With a deep breath, I walk towards the door and push it open.

Here goes nothing.

Chapter 3
SAM

The fluorescent lights flicker behind my closed eyes.

The sound is too loud to ignore, making sleep impossible. With a sigh, I open my eyes and attempt to stand.

My entire body aches from so many nights on the cold, hard floor.

Looking down and cringing at the effort it takes to simply move my neck, I see the scabs on my dirty skin and my overgrown nails. They're so long, it makes walking painful.

My fur is matted and dirty. I can't even remember what color I used to be. The shelter tries to let us out a few times a day, but when they get busy, we have to go to the bathroom in our kennels.

A pile of poop and a puddle of pee sits in one corner. I try to keep it far away from me, but there isn't much space.

The only thing I can smell is the ever-present odor that has probably seeped into my pores by now.

I don't know what's dirt and what's the stain of my own excrement, but I can't even bring myself to care or be disgusted. It's been my situation for too long to even have any feelings about it. This is my life; there is no other option.

Every movement is painful, but I shift so I'm facing away from the bars of my jail cell, hoping to block out the light now illuminating my pathetic 5x5 life.

I don't want anyone to see me like this.

I used to hope they would see me, but now, I only feel shame and despair.

I try and drift back to sleep, knowing I won't hear the creak of my cell door opening. It doesn't work. As I hear the door in the hallway shut softly, I realize I'm going to be spending another day staring at dark grey cement, counting the cracks in the walls for the 400th time.

Chapter 4
ROSIE

It's like walking into a wall of shit. Not really, but the smell is so bad, it might as well be. Cries and pleas loud enough to make my ears bleed reverberate down long hallway. There must be over 100 tiny cells running down the length of the building.

I understand how they feel.

As I find myself slowly walking down the row and looking at all the dirty faces, I realize I'm in a cage with each of them too; a prisoner to my stupid fucking brain.

The dogs look at me with desperation, so much so that I begin to cry.

My soul rots inside me each and every day—just like these little faces. They don't have much hope either; I can see it in their eyes, see it as they sit on the cold cement floor, covered in their own shit and piss, gaunt from hunger and sickness.

They are me and I am them.

Each and every one of them are reflections of what I'm becoming.

I'm breaking.

I'm broken.

Shattered in a thousand, jagged pieces on the dirty cement floor.

Three cells in, and I have to stop. It's too much. I don't think I can keep going. It hurts too much to see this pain, to realize how much pain I'm really in, to feel something other than numbness. I can hear my therapist in my head repeating "let's take some deep breaths" in a calm voice. Like taking a stupid breath is going to solve all my problems. Yeah, *sure*. Still, I don't really know what else to do right now except take some deep breaths. I made it this far; I have to keep going. That would just give me another reason to hate myself, an addition to my long list of *"Things Rosie has failed at."*

Inhale. *Fear.*

Exhale. *Keep going.*

Inhale. *Doubt.*

Exhale. *Keep walking.*

"You can do this, Rosie girl," I hear my mom's voice again.

But I...I don't know if I *can.*

Chapter 5
SAM

Footsteps echo around my cell. I can hear shuffling next door to me as my neighbor comes to attention, obviously having just awakened from a nap. I can hear him—or her; I don't really know, to be honest—walk to the front of his cement prison, towards the bars that lead to the hallway.

I consider it, I do. I glance to the front of my cell, at those silver bars, looking at the short walk it would take to get there. I'm just too tired, too achy. I can't remember the last time I had edible food. I can't even remember the last thing I ate.

I feel more lethargic than usual today. Oddly, it gives me a sad kind of hope. Maybe I'm coming to the end of my misery; maybe tomorrow will finally be the day this all comes to an end and I'm granted relief. I try not to dwell too long on that hope, resting my head back down and forsaking the idea of the short walk to the front of my cell. There is no point. I'd rather lie here. Really, I would. I push my head against the corner wall and turn my nose into my arm, not even attempting to get comfortable—it never works anyway.

Click, clack.

Click, clack.

Click, clack.

The footsteps get closer as I listen from my corner, the rhythmic pattern almost soothing.

They won't stop for me, I tell myself. *They never do.*

Chapter 6
ROSIE

Almost there, almost there. I'm almost to the end of the hallway, and then this will all be over. Then, I can go home and pretend this never happened. I can go back to my small, one bedroom apartment, where I spend most of my time in my bed staring at my ceiling or sleeping.

Even thinking about it makes me tired. I'm always exhausted nowadays. Even if I've slept for over 2 hours or 12, I'll walk up tired. Just a trip to the grocery store drains my energy completely. It's hard to explain, for people to understand. It's not just a physical exhaustion, like most people feel at the end of the day. It's an emotional exhaustion, a soul-deep exhaustion I feel down into my bones and in the crevices of my thump-thumping heart.

One more cage to pass.

One left to go.

Quickly walking past the cage at the end of the hall, I begin to turn to race back to my car when I stop, something catching my eye.

Chapter 7
SAM

The footsteps stop outside of my cell.

Go away. Stop tricking me.

Chapter 8
ROSIE

The dog is a brown lump in the corner, but this is the only one I've passed who didn't come to the front of the cage to greet me.

I understand why you won't get up, buddy. That's how I feel every morning.

I should go back to my car. My feet won't move, though.

Because I understand.

I don't know why, but something pulls me towards the creature.

I read the sign on the front of the door.

SAM

DAYS IN SHELTER: 1000

I nearly throw up. A thousand days in the shelter? I'm no math expert, but that's almost three years. *Three. Years.*

My soul *aches* just thinking about it.

With a deep breath, I slowly reach a hand up and unlatch the door to his kennel.

Chapter 9
SAM

Wait, what...? The door just unlocked... I slowly and hesitantly raise my head off my paws and glance around to look. A sad looking girl with big blue eyes gently steps inside my cage and bends down. Her eyes remind me of my own; they look how I feel. Hopeless, sad, tired.

I understand how you feel. I know why your eyes look that way.

Why are you here? I want to ask.

I try not to hope about what her presence means. Surely, she will see I'm broken and leave.

Surely.

Chapter 10
ROSIE

As I step into the cell, the lump raises its head slowly, as if in pain, and looks right into my eyes, as if it's seeing into my very soul, seeing my pain.

I'm surprised as bright blue eyes meet my own. I let out a chuckle, to my own surprise, and a little smile—it's the first time I've smiled in days.

We match. Sam's eyes are the same shade of blue as my own.

How funny.

I crouch down against the wall, giving him space but lowering myself to his level so I don't scare him.

For a while, Sam doesn't move. He simply watches me, shivering from the safety of his corner.

But he doesn't take his eyes off me.

"Hi Sam," I whisper. "My name is Rosie. It's nice to meet you."

Chapter 11
SAM

Rosie.

She's...*talking* to me.

"You look sad. I get that." She pauses. "I'm sad too."

She's sad too?

Her voice is soothing and soft, making me have feel something I haven't felt in a long time.

Safe.

Love.

"Don't be scared." I stare at her with rapt attention. "I won't hurt you, Sam. I'm here because I'm looking for a...well, a friend, honestly. I'm a little bit like you—sad and lonely. Most days, I want to give up."

Rosie pauses, and I watch as tears stream down her cheeks. She sniffs and wipes them away with the back of her hand.

"I bet you know how that feels, huh?"

I'm not really sure what to do, so I just keep staring. She's being nice to me. She's...not scary. I don't even know how to react, what the normal response would be.

But something sparks within me.

Something that feels terribly like *hope*.

Chapter 12
ROSIE

He's watching me, blue eyes the only clean thing on him. His fur is full of matts and dirt, so much so that I'm not even sure what color he is. He keeps staring at me, making no move to come over to me.

I get it, buddy. I'm sorry...

I've been sitting on the floor with him for a while, but he's still just in his corner, watching me. Slowly, I reluctantly get up and turn to walk out, knowing he doesn't want my help—he doesn't *want* me.

But suddenly, a cold, wet nose nudges my hand, and I gasp.

Chapter 13
SAM

Don't go. Please... I saw her start to leave, and suddenly, my weary legs were upright and I was padding over to her, not knowing what else to do but nudge her odd, bald paw to try and stop her. I'm a little shaky now that I'm fully standing, but for the first time in who knows how long, I have a reason to keep fighting, to keep standing and keep going.

"You...don't want me to leave?" She bends down so we're eye to eye.

I lick her check, and she giggles.

"Okay. Okay, buddy. I'll tell you what."

She's leaving me, isn't she? I look down at the floor, knowing her response.

"I'm gonna leave," *I knew it,* "but what would you think about leaving with me?"

I'm...leaving with you?

"Would you like that?" she asks, her eyes glassy and full of tears even though she's smiling.

She's smiling at *me*.

I lick her cheek again and *woof* lightly. Not to scare her, but because I want her to know that yes, yes, I *do* want to go home with her.

I never thought this day would come, that this could be possible.

"I'll take that as a yes," she laughs. "I think our first stop will be the groomer, and I'll get all this dirt off you, okay?"

I *woof* again. Yes, *please.* I want to be clean!

"I'm not the most interesting person," Rosie admits, petting my head. I melt into her touch. It feels like with every stroke of her hand, my tension eases away. "But I can promise I will always be there for you. I will always take care of you, and I will never leave you. We'll go on walks and play with toys, and you can help me with my homework. Does that sound good?"

My tail wags so hard, I nearly pull a muscle.

"Okay then." Rosie smiles. "Let's get out of here, Sam."

I'm leaving.

I'm leaving! I'm finally leaving! I get to have a home!

Chapter 14

ROSIE

"We're gonna be best friends, alright? We'll help each other to not feel sad." If dogs could cry, I think that's what he started doing. His head leans into my chest, pressing into me as if he needs me like he needs his next breath.

I'm crying too, understanding how he feels. I've only known him for a few minutes, a mere fraction of a lifetime, yet I feel like he's my oxygen, like my entire universe suddenly shifted to revolve around him. It's funny how quickly things like this can happen.

There's no collar, no leash to lead him out, but I just get this feeling he's not going to dash out once we leave the cage. I walk, and he follows me down the hall, staying right by my side and pressing into my leg. I keep my hand on his neck—not to control or punish, but because touching him, feeling his warm fur...it makes me feel happy.

It makes me feel *safe*.

We fill out more paperwork and get a stupid little "congratulations on your adoption!" sticker. There are a few collars and leashes for purchase behind the counter, so I pick plain black and then turn to leave once he's all set.

"He's our longest resident," the woman says quietly, tears in her eyes. "I've been hoping someone would see how much love he has to give. I'm so happy you found each other."

Strangely, I smile and admit, "I am too."

"Are you going to keep his name?" she asks.

I nod. "Yeah. He seems like a Sam to me."

"Well then." The woman looks down at Sam. "Enjoy your new life, Sam. You're going *home*."

Chapter 15
SAM

The car ride felt like heaven.

I watch as buildings pass in wonder.

We stop at a place with bathtubs meant for dogs, and Rosie is so gentle, so careful to help me up the ramp and into the bathtub.

She even waits for the water to get warm before soaking my fur. It feels so nice, I lay down in the tub as she rinses me. Pain leaves my muscles as I soak, and she begins massaging soap into my fur.

"Oh my God, Sam! You're white!" I glance down at my paws covered in dirty but warm water. My fur *is* gleaming white.

Now, I remember.

She rinses out the shampoo and then puts something called "conditioner" in my fur, which smells yummy and makes me real soft.

When that's rinsed, Rosie dries me off with a towel before clipping my long nails. My paws feel so much better now. I cover her face with kisses, causing more giggles, which are quickly becoming my favorite sound.

She lets me climb out of the bath, and I stand patiently while she uses some sort of machine that blows warm air on my fur. It feels so good.

Now, I'm clean and dry, my fur fluffed to perfection. I can't stop looking at Rosie. I don't want her to stop touching me.

After the bath, Rosie takes me to a little area with toys and beds. She lets me pick out three toys and my own bed.

A bed. Just for me.

I can't believe it.

I pick the softest one, and she checks out, purchasing my new goodies. It feels like a dream.

We get back into her car and drive for a while before pulling up to a small house.

This is all for me?

This is my home?

I walk right beside her as we enter the home, looking around in awe.

"Well, welcome home, Sam. What do you think?" Rosie asks. I can sense she's nervous, so I lick her hand, and she sighs in relief. "Oh, good."

Rosie feeds me dinner and pours some warm liquid on top of it that smells delicious.

Chicken broth, I think she called it.

It was so good, I ate two servings.

Rosie sits on the floor with me, eating her own dinner, while I stretch out and digest mine. My belly feels so wonderful and *full.*

"You're never going to be hungry again. I promise, Sam."

I believe her. I once again lean against her leg as we walk to her bedroom after she finishes eating.

Climbing up onto the bed, I make a few circles next to her as she lays down before pressing myself against her side.

The bed is so soft. There are so many warm blankets.

I glance at Rosie, who's currently making sure I'm comfortable, putting a pillow under my head so we're face to face under the covers.

Thank you for saving me. I'm exhausted and my eyes are shutting. I wish I could tell her this, tell her how thankful I am for her, how I never thought I would feel this safe or happy again. I forgot what it even felt like.

Chapter 16
ROSIE

Sam, who shockingly turned out to be a gorgeous, pure white mutt of some kind, sits on the pillows next to me, looking warm and happy for the first time in God knows how long.

I can't believe he had to live in that shelter. It makes me so angry to think about, but he's home now.

He's free, and that makes me so happy.

The phone rings, and Sam opens his eyes as I reach over and grab it.

"Hi, sweetie!" my mom says. "How did it go? Did you find a buddy?"

I pull the phone away from my ear and snap a quick picture of Sam before sending it to her.

"Check your messages," I laugh. I can hear the gasp as my mom looks at the photo.

"Oh, honey! He's so beautiful. What's his name?"

"Sam," I answer. "His name is Sam."

Hearing his name, Sam licks my hand, and I laugh. My mom laughs too, elated to hear the sound.

"I'm so happy for you, honey. You sound so happy too. I'm so glad you rescued Sam, and I'm so proud of you for going to the shelter. You were really brave today and look what happened. You *saved* him."

The words make me smile, but they're not completely true.

Yes, I saved him...but he saved *me* too.

"Thanks, Mom. I'm happy too. I didn't think it would work out, but the moment I saw him... I don't know. It just felt right. It *feels* right."

My mom and I chat for a while as she and my dad cook dinner.

I can't even remember the first time I felt anything other than sadness, but as my new furry companion drifts to sleep peacefully next to me, I can't help but feel something new.

Love.

Happiness.

Hope.

I say goodbye to my parents and put on a movie, snuggling up to Sam, who is snoring lightly, his head pressed into my chest and his paws tucked up, turning him into a little donut.

"I know people may think I saved you," I whisper to him, pressing a kiss against his soft cheek, "but it's *you* who saved *me,*

Sam. Thank you for picking me. I will love you for the rest of your life. I promise."

And I do.

THANK YOU

Something about me is that I always start my acknowledgements by thanking the animals who have saved my life. With this story, it feels particularly important to do so. When the depression makes everything seem hopeless, and when my anxiety makes me too scared to move, the love of animals always brings me back into the light.

Boomer, Luca, Flynn, Beau, Blue, Xena, Stanley, Tosh, Artemis, Sophie, Jinx, Derek, Manny, BB, Stormy, Lady... I could go on. **Frankie,** thank you for being my best friend, even if it ended up that I'm your Emotional Support Human instead of you being my Emotional Support Animal. I never thought I could love something as much as I love you. Thank you for always licking up my tears and loving me more than anything on this planet. I hope this book sheds some light on the ways animals are suffering; and how, even in the face of cruelty, they have so much love to give us. They deserve our respect and care in return.

Mom and Dad, thank you for always supporting me.

To the **Schaeffel Clan, Wolski Clan, and Garrett Clan,** thank you for making me feel like I'm not alone in this world.

Tiffany, Lyss, Corrine, Becky + DJ, Reina, Beth, Lindsay, Marilu, Rachel, Alexa, Gabi, & Esther– I love you all so much and I'm so thankful to have you in my life. Distance and time will never push us apart.

Trash Bandits. Thank you for encouraging me to sprint even on the days when I don't feel like it. **CK Beggan, Reina, Trent, Lindsay, David, Ava Thorne, and Marilou Moser.** It's an honor to write alongside you all and to call you, my friends.

To my editor **Alexa/The Fiction Fix,** infinite thanks and gratitude for your friendship, mentorship, and your keen eye. You improved this story so much, and I am so thankful.

To **Under The Cover + Jess and Carley,** thank you for championing indie authors and for all of the support. You keep me going.

To the **University of Nevada, Reno, and the College of Liberal Arts.** This story was crafted in a creative writing class, and I'm endlessly grateful for what I learned from it. Thank you to everyone in that class for your feedback. Sharing stories is so vulnerable and it can be really scary, but you all made it a wonderful experience.

The Author

EC Garrett is an Alaskan transplant now living in Kansas City, MO who writes fantasy/sci-fi speculative fiction. She received her Bachelor's Degree in English Literature with a focus in Early Modern and Medieval Literature and a minor in Medieval History from the University of Nevada, Reno in 2016. ECG is currently attending the University of Missouri-Kansas City where she is working on her Masters in English literature. In her spare time, she's either reading or watching the latest fantasy releases, riding horses at the barn, spending time with her family, or playing with her very cute but extremely ornery dachshund mix, Frankie.

She dreams of becoming a dragon rider.

Follow ECG on social media to get all the latest updates.

www.authorecgarrett.com

Instagram: @authorecgarrett

Tiktok: @author.ecgarrett

Threads: @authorecgarrett

Facebook: @authorecgarrett

Also by EC Garrett

<u>REPUBLICA HELVETORUM</u>

gothic monster romance

Here There Be Monsters

Here There Be Witches – *coming mid 2025*

There Are Monsters Beneath – *coming late 2025*

<u>THE DRAGON QUEEN</u>

dark epic fantasy

The Forgotten and The Feared

The Broken and The Brave

The Defiant and The Damned – *coming 2/25/25*

TDQ3 – *coming late 2025/early 2026*

<u>THE HOME FOR WAYWARD CREATURES</u>

paranormal romantic sci-fi

Vol. 1 – *coming spring 2025*

Vol. 2 – *coming 2026*

<u>SHORT STORIES</u>

Rescue Me – *contemporary fiction*

Fury – sci-fi body horror– coming 2025

Midnight Pages

indie publishing house + bookish candles
handmade in kansas city, mo